To Aaron, who asked me to write a book he could read,
and later helped edit it.

.•Contents•.

Fowl Language

Starring...

Ashley
Dave
Benny
And introducing...
Ed
The Supernatural Rubber Chicken!

Chapter 1
Dave Leaves.
The Rubber Chicken Stays.

Ten-year-old twins Nate and Lisa Zupinski walked into their house together after school.

Nate slammed the front door, threw down his dirty gray backpack, and kicked it toward the hall closet. "What an awful day!" he yelled.

"You don't have to yell," Lisa said. "But it was a terrible day." She gently placed her pretty pink princess backpack inside the closet.

Their mother stopped typing on the computer. "Did you have a good day?" she asked.

"No," Lisa said. "Our teacher Mrs. Crabpit smelled horrible. Even for *her*. I had to keep tissues stuffed up my nostrils."

"How sweet," their mother said as she stared at the computer screen. She wrote

FUFU
FALLS
ASLEEP

award-winning children's books which children had to be forced to read.

"Hulk Paine said he'd trade me something for my new pencil," Nate said. "So I gave him my pencil. In exchange, he gave me a wedgie and three noogies."

"What a generous friend," their mother said.

The twins' older brother, Dave, woke up from his snooze on the couch and took *Surferdude Magazine* off his face. "I'm leaving home to ride the waves on far off shores," he announced.

Their mother said, "Lovely," and resumed typing.

Nate asked Dave where he was going.

"To ride the waves on far off shores, dude."

"You already said that," Nate said.

Dave shook his head. "I didn't say 'dude' before."

"But what shores?" Lisa asked.

"Far off ones," Dave said.

"Fiji? Thailand?" Nate asked. "Australia?"

"Malibu, California. It's a five-hour drive from Boring."

Dave meant Boring, Arizona, where the Zupinski family lived. He didn't mean *Man, this town is boring*, even though usually it was.

Dave suddenly stood up and ran to his bedroom. He shouted, "Dudes! I totally forgot to show you something! Come in here."

Nate and Lisa slowly walked toward

Dave's room. They knew they had to be very careful in there.

"I think I hear a mouse by the bedroom door," Lisa whispered.

Nate's face collided with a gigantic spiderweb hanging from the doorway.

"Like, check it out." Dave pointed to his bed (unmade, of course).

Nate and Lisa tiptoed over to it. It was a hard journey. Dave's floor was covered with Twinkie wrappers, sunblock tubes, a backpack, a wetsuit, and a stretchy, stinky string of seaweed.

A pile of dirty clothes lay in the center of the bed. On top of the pile was a filthy, old, and extremely ugly rubber chicken.

"Eww," Lisa said.

"You should think about getting a trash can," Nate said.

"Dudes, I don't have time for that," Dave said. "Far off shores are calling. **'Dave, Dave, DAVE!'** "

"I don't hear anything," Nate said.

"I do," Lisa said. "I hear a voice calling, **'Dave, Dave, DAVE!** Get rid of that nasty rubber chicken before it gives someone bird flu!'"

Dave pinched her cheek. "You kids are adorable, but I have waves to ride. Just take good care of the chicken. He's yours now."

Lisa made a face. "I don't want that yucky thing. Nate can have it."

"No thanks. That chicken is foul." Nate chuckled. "Get it? *Foul* means something bad and *fowl* means a bird. Get it?"

Dave scratched his head.

Lisa asked if she could have Dave's video games instead.

"Dudes," Dave said. "This is a Super-natural rubber chicken."

Nate and Lisa rolled their eyes. They knew their brother Dave was a bit dim, but they never thought he was dim enough to believe a rubber chicken was supernatural.

"Like, really," Dave said. "The chicken is

magic. I found him on a beach in Honolulu. See the lei he's wearing?"

Nate peered at the rubber chicken again. "You mean that green necklace around its ugly neck?" he asked.

"Don't call it a necklace. It's a Hawaiian lei." Dave put his hand on the green necklace. "And don't insult his neck. The rubber chicken is very sensitive about his looks."

"How could a toy be sensitive?" Lisa asked.

"The chicken isn't a toy. I mean, he's a real rubber chicken," Dave said. "When I first saw him washed up on the beach, I thought he was dead. I was, like, how sad, a dead little chicken dude. But then he started talking."

Nate shook his head. "How dumb do you think we are?"

"Don't answer that," Lisa said.

"Seriously, the chicken talks." Dave lifted it by its long, bumpy neck. Its flabby body hung limp. It didn't talk, or even squawk.

"Eww," Lisa said again.

"So what does the chicken say?" Nate asked. "'Here's the real reason I crossed the road'? Or does it only talk to its friends Henny Penny and Donald Duck?"

Dave pinched Nate's cheek. "Dude, I have to go. The chicken is supernatural. He's, like, magic. He'll give the first person who touches him a superpower. And you guys get to pick which power. Tell him, like, 'You will

9

provide the next dude or dudette with super strength.' The power lasts only a day or two. And let the chicken rest in between wishes. Even supernatural rubber chickens need a break now and then."

"Have you been surfing in polluted water again?" Lisa asked.

"Hey, if the chicken's so magical, why don't you make it give you the power to fly to California?" Nate asked.

"The superpowers don't work on his owners. Duh!" Dave said. "Plus, there's no room for him in my backpack. But trust me, this chicken is awesome. Just remember: Sometimes his spells don't seem to work out, but they always do in the end."

Dave grabbed his wetsuit and back-pack from the rug, and walked out of the bedroom, past his mother at the computer, and out the front door.

Chapter 2
It Talks!

Lisa and Nate ran to their mother and shouted, "Mom! Dave is leaving for California!"

"That's nice, dears," she said. "What should I name the dog in my new novel? Sweetums? Cupcake? Angel?"

Nate groaned. "You're writing another dead dog book?"

Their dog, Plop, who had been sprawled under their mother's chair, whimpered.

In their mother's last book, *Tina and Fufu*, the dog rescued Tina's family from a fire before dying of smoke inhalation. Before that, in *Steven and Spot*, Spot saved Steven from a runaway motorcycle, but broke all four of his legs. And before that, in *The Evil Terrorists and Their Cute Dog Fluffy*, the dog lived but the cat died.

"How about the name Rover?" their mother asked.

"Mom! Dave is gone!" Lisa exclaimed.

"Maybe something exotic like Beyoncé," their mother said.

"He gave us his supernatural rubber chicken," Nate said.

"Great suggestion. A supernatural dog."

Ms. Zupinski beamed. "A supernatural dog story might finally win me the Newbery award! I'll make two dogs die this time."

Plop growled and bit her tail. She wasn't exactly the world's smartest dog. Then she settled on the rug and started snoring. She wasn't exactly the world's liveliest dog either. In fact, she was the world's laziest dog.

The twins returned to Dave's room. On the way, Lisa got two more tissues to plug up her nostrils.

They approached the bed and stared at the rubber chicken.

"It's so gross," Lisa said.

A loud, scratchy voice squawked, "Who are you calling gross, girlie? What's gross is this sweaty underwear your brother Dave dumped me on."

The voice seemed to be coming from the chicken, which was in fact lying on a pair of smelly underwear.

"Ding-dong, dumb Dave is gone," the voice said. "If a bird had his brain, it would fly backwards."

Nate was so shocked, he couldn't even speak.

Neither could Lisa, though her mouth hung wide open.

"Close your mouth before someone

puts an apple in it," the chicken screeched. "And get me off of Dave's dirty underwear!"

Nate grabbed the chicken by one of its feet and moved it to Dave's pillow.

"This pillowcase is almost as dirty as the underwear," the chicken said. **"P.U.!"**

"You. . . you. . . you're. . ." Nate couldn't finish his sentence.

Lisa's mouth had opened even wider, but she was still speechless.

"Sheesh! You two are even dumber than your brother," the chicken said. "And people say chickens are stupid."

Nate thought about calling his friends to show off the talking rubber chicken.

Lisa wondered if she could sell it on the Internet.

But all they could do was stare.

"So you both own me now, huh?" the chicken said. "Whose room am I sleeping in tonight? Dave's room is a pig sty."

Nate and Lisa stared at each other, then stared at the chicken, then stared at each other again.

"Hurry up and get me out of here! I'm sick of looking at surfing posters and smelling seaweed and dirty clothes."

"Darn. I think I hear my mother calling me," Lisa said.

"What? She never calls us," Nate said.

Lisa left the room.

"Ohh, I hear her calling, too," Nate lied. "Bye."

"You're going to leave me here?" the chicken asked. "To rot on this horrible pillowcase, surrounded by greasy blond hairs and wet sand? After all I've done for your dumb brother?"

"Yep. Bye-bye," Nate said. He rushed out of the room and closed the door behind him.

Chapter 3

Adventures in Long Division

At school the next day, Nate and Lisa almost forgot about the rubber chicken. Their teacher, Mrs. Crabpit, could make people forget about everything except how stinky she was. And how mean she was.

Mrs. Crabpit stood in front of the class with her arms crossed. "Who would like to go to the whiteboard and solve this easy math problem?" she asked.

$$8{,}829 \overline{)267{,}431}$$

No one else in the classroom thought dividing 267,431 by 8,829 was easy.

So they looked away. They knew the secret to avoid being called on in class: Refuse to meet the teacher's eyes and try not to seem too worried. Take your mind off the fact that the world's nastiest teacher was

trying to choose her next victim.

Lisa thought about Mr. Crabpit. If there was a *Mrs.* Crabpit, Lisa figured there must be a *Mr.* Crabpit. She wondered if he was mean and stinky too. Or perhaps he was nice, but Mrs. Crabpit kept him locked up in their smelly house so he couldn't escape.

Imagining Mrs. Crabpit's house was too scary. Lisa glanced around the room to think about her classmates instead. Brittany Billingsworth was so nervous, her face was covered with a rash. Michael Perez's face was covered with gobs of sweat.

They and everyone else in the class had caught on to the secret, and weren't looking at the teacher either. Except for Benny B. Benjamin, but he didn't catch on to much of anything. He was staring right into Mrs. Crabpit's eyes.

"Benny," the teacher said with a thin smile.

He tilted his head. "Huh?"

"Come up to the board and solve the problem."

"What? Me? Now?" he asked.

Behind him, Hulk Paine whispered evilly, "You'll never figure it out, dumbhead."

Benny slowly made his way to the whiteboard. He stared at the long division problem. He moved to the side and peered at it from an angle. He moved to the other side and peered at it from another angle.

He shrugged.

He tapped his foot.

He accidentally stubbed his toe.

Mrs. Crabpit sighed. "Benny, Benny, Benny."

"You're talking about me, right?" Benny asked.

"Who else would like to volunteer?" the

teacher said, her eyes narrowed to thin slits, her mouth turned down in a major frown.

The class quickly returned to no-eye-contact mode.

"Ashley. You." Mrs. Crabpit pointed at Ashley Chang.

Lisa stared at her friend. Ashley's cheeks got about as red as Rudolph the Reindeer's nose.

Lisa didn't used to believe the story of Rudolph the Red-nosed Reindeer. But after hearing a rubber chicken talk yesterday, she now believed in Rudolph, leprechauns, the Easter Bunny, and that if she swallowed a cherry pit, a tree would grow inside her stomach.

"Hurry up, Ashley," Mrs. Crabpit said.

Ashley slowly walked to the board.

Hulk whispered, "Let's see if Scaredy-pants can help Stupid-boy."

"Shh!" Lisa and Nate both hissed.

Benny and Ashley stood at the board together, in total silence.

Benny wrinkled his eyebrows.

Ashley wrote numbers on the board and then erased them.

Mrs. Crabpit put her hands on her hips. "Didn't you learn long division in kindergarten?"

Benny shrugged.

Ashley's cheeks got even redder.

Mrs. Crabpit raised her arm and flung the back of her hand onto her forehead as if she had a headache. Her stinky odor went through the roof.

It really did. In fact, birds on the roof flew away as fast as they could. One pigeon was so sickened by Mrs. Crabpit's smell that it threw up on the bald head of Mr. Song, the music teacher. Mr. Song took that as a sign that he should quit teaching and form a rock band called Barf.

But everyone inside Mrs. Crabpit's classroom just took her bad smell as a sign that she needed a shower. They couldn't wait to leave.

Chapter 4
Wanted: One Rubber Chicken

The bell rang. Mrs. Crabpit told her students, "Go. Just get out of here."

Benny walked off, and Nate put his arm around him as they left the classroom.

Ashley walked off, and Lisa put her arm around her as they left the classroom.

Hulk stood at the doorway, calling everyone mean names such as doofus and dodo-brain, and trying to trip them with his huge foot.

Outside, Lisa sat next to Ashley and carefully took her strawberry yogurt out of her pink plush lunch box. "Are you all right?" Lisa asked her friend.

Ashley shook her head.

"Don't feel bad," Lisa said as she ate a tiny spoonful of yogurt. "No one could have solved that long division problem in such a short amount of time."

"Thanks," Ashley whispered in a shaky voice.

Across the table, Nate shoved half his baloney/ham/roast beef sandwich into his mouth.

"Doh fee bad," he told Benny with his mouth bursting with meat, white bread, ketchup, onions, and seven pickle slices. He finished his sandwich with a loud gulp. "That math problem was horrible."

"It sure was," Benny said.

Lisa sipped on her pink lemonade. She told Ashley, "I have just the thing to turn a bad day into a great one. Let's go to the mall. We can try on some pretty, puffy, pink party dresses. Shopping always makes me forget my problems."

Nate gobbled up his kingsize chocolate-peanut butter-marshmallow brownie in two bites. Then he told Benny, "I know how to make things better. Handball. Think of it: running around and hitting hardies, babies, deadmen, slicers, and sliders. Your day will turn right around."

Hulk Paine walked over to their table. "You know what they call people who don't talk?" he asked Ashley. "Dumb, that's what. Dumb, dumb, dumb. And you know what they call you, Benny? Dumb, that's what. Dumb, dumb, dumb."

"Shut up, jerkface," Nate said.

"Please be quiet, jerkface," Lisa said.

Hulk jabbed his huge finger into Nate's cheek. "You have brown things in your teeth and all over your face. You're a disgusting pig."

"Those brown things are either meat shreds or smushed brownie or both. Thanks for letting me know." Nate put his tongue out and licked as much off his face as he could.

"Mmm. A tasty beef-brownie combo. By the way, Hulk, name-calling doesn't hurt me."

"Lisa, you are an annoying buttinski," Hulk said.

"Names will never hurt me," Lisa replied.

"Nate, I let all the air out of the handballs so you can't play today," Hulk said.

Nate gasped in horror.

"And, Lisa, your dress is out of style," Hulk said. "That powder pink paisley look is totally three months ago. I'm going to report you to the fashion police."

Lisa clutched her heart.

Hulk walked away.

Ashley and Benny plunked their faces on the lunch table.

Nate muttered, "Not the handballs. Not the handballs."

Lisa stared down at her dress and shook her head.

Nate and Lisa both said at the same time, "Tomorrow, I'm going to bring the super-natural rubber chicken to school."

Chapter 5
Rubber Chicken on the Loose

As soon as the school bus dropped off Nate and Lisa at their stop, they raced home. They both really wanted the chicken.

Well, they didn't really want the chicken. Because who wants a rubber chicken with a bad attitude? Nate liked his handball a lot better. Lisa would have preferred a supernatural teddy bear.

But they both wanted to use the rubber

chicken's supernatural powers. And they both knew they had to get to the chicken first.

As they ran, they heard a dog barking. It sounded as if it was coming from their house.

"Could that be Plop?" Nate asked Lisa as she ran next to him.

"No. That's impossible," she said. "Plop is an old, lazy dog who hasn't barked in years."

"Maybe Miss McKendry's bulldog is chasing down the Girl Scouts again," Nate said.

"Or it could be Pudge Wilcox's schnauzer trying to tackle his shadow again," Lisa suggested.

"But it sounds like it's coming from our house," Nate said.

"Well, it couldn't be our dog," Lisa said. "Plop doesn't bark. She hardly does anything. Mostly, Plop plops."

Nate made it into Dave's old bedroom first.

The chicken was not on Dave's pillow—former pillow, actually—where they had left it.

Lisa arrived a few moments later. She stood in the doorway with her hands over her face to fight off the spiderwebs. "Did you take the chicken?" she asked Nate.

"Not me. Did you take it?"

"Eww. No way," Lisa said.

Meanwhile, a dog in the backyard was barking like crazy. The twins didn't take the time to check whether it was Plop. They had a rubber chicken to find.

Nate made a clucking noise. "He-e-ere, chicky chicky! Come on out wherever you are!"

There was no response. Not a squawk, not a cluck, not even a **Shut up, you knuckle-heads, I'm trying to sleep.**

"Chicken? Oh rub-ber chic-ken," Lisa called out. "I understand if you're trying to hide from Nate. He can be really annoying. Plus, he's almost as big a slob as our brother Dave." She inched forward. "You can hang out with me instead, sweet little chicken. You should see my room. It's sparkling clean."

"But it's pink. Very, very pink," Nate pointed out. "My room is a manly shade of beige."

"Chickens don't care about manly shades. They're not men. They're chickens, for your information," Lisa said.

"Okay," Nate said. "Then my room's a chicken-ly shade of beige. Just like a chicken coop on a farm."

Lisa put her hands on her hips. "Just to let you know, Mr. Rubber Chicken, Nate's never been on a farm in his life."

"Neither has Lisa." Nate lifted the pillow and peered underneath.

"Yeah, but I read *Charlotte's Web,* which is set on a farm," Lisa said.

"Well, I saw the movie version," Nate said. "Lisa might have a lot of books in her room, but I have more video games." He looked under the bed.

Meanwhile, the dog in the backyard kept barking.

Lisa and Nate searched all over Dave's room. The only inter-esting thing they found was half a green-and-black sprinkled donut in Dave's sock drawer.

"Mmm, I love donuts with sprinkles." Nate put it up to his mouth.

"No!" Lisa shouted. "Those aren't sprinkles!"

"Then what are those little black and green things?" Nate asked.

"Ants and mold," Lisa said.

"Yikes!" Nate shoved the donut back into the sock drawer. He could still hear the dog's loud barking. "That noise is driving me crazy," he said. "I'm going to find out whose dog that is."

"I need to get out of here too," Lisa said. "Dave's room is disgusting. I'll be in the bathroom washing my hands for about an hour. I wish I knew what happened to that rubber chicken."

Chapter 6

Plop Doesn't Plop

When Nate opened the door to the back-yard, he almost collapsed from shock. The barking dog was Plop!

Nate let the dog into the house, but that didn't calm her down. Not only did Plop keep barking, she started jumping all over the sofa.

"Down, girl!" Nate yelled.

So the dog got down from the sofa and jumped all over Nate.

Nate shouted, "**Ack!** Yowza! Help! **Stop! Yikes!**" and so on, including one nasty word he'd learned yesterday from a fifth-grader on the school bus.

Lisa rushed into the room. "Are you okay?" she asked Nate.

Meanwhile, their mother sat at the computer, typing and muttering, "Must win Newbery Award, must win Newbery Award."

Plop jumped on Lisa and licked her like she was a melting ice cream cone.

"Eww. I just spent a long time washing my hands," Lisa said. "Now I have to wash them again, plus my face, and my arms, and everything else Plop's yucky tongue landed on."

"What has gotten into our dog?" Nate asked. "Do you even remember the last time Plop barked, jumped, or stood up to lick the toilet bowl?"

"I was wondering the same thing," Lisa said. "Except for the toilet bowl licking, because that grosses me out."

"It's like she has super strength or something," Nate said.

Nate and Lisa stared at each other.

Mrs. Zupinski kept staring at her computer.

"Uh oh," the twins both said. "Super strength. The supernatural rubber chicken made Plop super strong!"

"Ruff, ruff, ruff," Plop barked.

"Yes, that is rough." Mrs. Zupinski nodded. "It would be rough to write a book about a supernatural chicken, because that will never win a Newbery Award."

She suddenly stopped typing and snapped her fingers. "Unless the chicken dies at the end of the book. Or his friend the dog dies. Or a mother dies. Ooh! What if the dog's mother died after eating spoiled chicken? Yes! That sounds like an award-winning book." She continued typing, faster than ever now.

Plop ran out the door to the backyard again.

Nate and Lisa followed her.

"So you think . . ." Lisa started.

"Plop touched the chicken?" Nate continued.

"And got super strength, just like Dave said?" Lisa asked.

Nate nodded. "Enough strength to dig holes all over our backyard."

They both stared at the grassy yard. It was now full of deep holes. The holes in the yard looked like something a normal dog would take a year to do. (Not that a normal dog would be allowed to dig up a backyard like that.)

And Plop was still digging. Quickly, deeply, and noisily. "It's like she's turned into Superdog or something," Nate said.

"More like Super-awful-dog," Lisa added.

"Do you think Plop could have buried the chicken in one of those holes?"

Instead of answering, Nate ran to the nearest hole and peered in.

He spied dirt, rocks, and a big mound of fresh dog doo. But he didn't see a rubber chicken. Drat! He had to have that chicken so he could help his friend Benny.

Lisa ran to the second nearest hole and peered in.

"Darn! It's empty," she said. "I have to have that chicken so I can help my friend Ashley."

They both ran around the backyard looking into the holes. Meanwhile, Plop kept barking and digging more of them.

This went on for a long time.

A very long time.

As Dave would say, *Like, almost totally forever, dude.*

And after all that time, the twins still hadn't found the rubber chicken.

Chapter 7

Something Really Important

When it started to get dark and the twins were so exhausted they could barely stay standing, they returned to the house.

The phone was ringing. Nate answered it in the living room. "Hello?"

"Dude?"

"Dave!" Nate exclaimed.

Lisa ran to the bathroom and picked up the other phone. "Dave!" she yelled.

"Dudes," Dave said. "I spent all last night surfing. Then I spent all morning surfing. Then I spent all afternoon surfing. Guess what I'll be doing tonight?"

"Surfing?" Nate asked.

"Whoa," Dave said. "How did you know? Dude, you're, like, a genius. Talk to you later. Gotta catch some waves."

"Wait," Lisa said. "What about the rubber chicken?"

"I totally trust you guys. I'm sure my old chicken's in, like, good hands. Thanks for taking care of the little dude."

"You're welcome," Nate said with his teeth clenched.

"Oh, I forgot to tell you something totally

important," Dave said. He told them, but
Nate and Lisa couldn't hear over Plop's loud
barking.

"Keep Plop away from the chicken!"
Dave shouted. Then he said, "Hang ten," and
hung up the phone.

"Who was that?" their mother asked. "One of my fans?"

"No," Nate said. "That was your son, Dave."

"Oh. Did he say what time he'll be home?" their mother asked.

"He's gone," Lisa reminded her. "He's surfing the waves on far off shores."

"So will he be home for dinner?" she asked.

Nate sighed. "I don't think so."

Mrs. Zupinski shrugged and returned to her computer.

"How could we have lost the rubber chicken just one day after we got it?" Lisa said.

"Does that mean our surferdude brother is more responsible than us?" Nate asked.

"Maybe not," Lisa said. "Maybe he's just smarter."

"Dave? Smarter than us?" Nate asked.

Both twins shuddered.

Lisa shook her head. "That would be way too embarrassing."

"We'd better find that chicken," Nate said.

Chapter 8
Eureka!

Nate and Lisa stood in the backyard holding flashlights, on another round of rubber chicken hunt.

"Any luck?" Nate asked as he put his hand into the zillionth hole of the night.

"What?" Lisa shouted over Plop's barks.

"I said, 'Any luck?'" Nate put his hand into the zillionth-and-first hole of the night.

Lisa shined her flashlight on her brother.

"I wish we could find that rubber chicken. I'm so tired of—Hey! I feel something in this hole!"

"What?" Nate asked.

"Something rubbery."

Nate walked over to Lisa. "Rubbery like a rubber chicken?"

"No, stupid, a rubber cow," the chicken said from inside the hole.

"Eureka!" Lisa yelled.

"Don't call me 'Eureka,'" the rubber chicken said. "That's a girl's name."

"Sorry," Lisa said. "But 'Eureka' means we're happy we found you."

"I never imagined I'd be so happy to see an old rubber chicken," Nate said.

"Well, I'm glad to see you too," the rubber

chicken said. "As long as you don't call me Eureka."

"So what should we call you?" Lisa asked.

"The name's Ed," the chicken said. "Now get me out of this hideous hole. Some time this week would be nice."

"Give us a break. We didn't know Plop would act like this," Nate said.

"She's a dog," the chicken said. "Dogs put things in their mouths and then bury them. Any idiot knows that."

Lisa smiled. "Then I guess we're not idiots because we didn't know that."

"So that means you're the only idiot here," Nate told Ed.

Plop jumped on Nate again.

"Besides Plop. She's an idiot too," Lisa said.

Plop put her nose into the hole and sniffed Ed excitedly.

"Help! Now!" Ed shouted. "Dummies!"

Lisa shined the flashlight on him. "If you're going to call us names, then just forget it. You can stay in here all night and think about being nice to others."

The chicken rolled his eyes.

"Wow! Cool!" Nate shouted. "You can talk and move!"

"I can only move my face a bit, unfortunately," Ed said. "If I could move my body, I would have been out of this hole hours ago, and on my way to a lavish vacation in the Bahamas. But instead, I have to wait for you two nincompoops to help me."

"Are you going to be nice to us or not?" Lisa asked him.

"Okay, okay. No more name-calling," Ed said. "Just get me away from your mangy mutt."

Plop started howling.

"And don't insult our dog," Nate said.

The chicken sighed. "Fine. Your idiotic mutt isn't mangy. Now get me out of here."

"What do you say?" Lisa asked.

"I say that I'd rather be on top of Dave's underwear again than buried in the backyard."

"No! That's not what you say. You're supposed to say 'please,'" Lisa told him. "Or you can say 'pretty please' or 'pretty please with sugar on top.'"

"Fine," Ed said. "Please."

Lisa pulled him out of the hole.

"It's about time," Ed complained.

"Eww," Lisa said. "You feel all slimy and you don't smell too good either."

"Your disgusting dog put me in her

slobbery mouth, and I've been lying in the dirt all day. What did you expect?"

"Poor Ed. You need a bath," Lisa told him.

Lisa loved giving baths. She bathed her dolls, her play jewelry, Nate's dinosaur collection, the silverware, the can opener, and her bicycle helmet.

"I'd rather have a shower," Ed said. "I'm a filthy mess. And It's all because of your brother, Dave, and your dog Plop. I hated granting Dave's wish to give the mutt super strength."

"So why did you do it?" Nate asked him.

"Because I had to," the rubber chicken said. "Once my owner makes a wish, I have to grant it. Even if my owner is a total dunce. No offense."

"No offense taken. That was a bad wish." Nate pointed to Plop, who was running in circles around them and barking.

"For the next wish, I want you to give my friend Ashley a superpower," Lisa told Ed.

"My friend Benny needs a superpower more," Nate argued.

"He does not," Lisa said.

"Does so," Nate said.

"Does not." Lisa stamped her foot.

"Does so." Nate stamped his foot.

"SHUT UP!" the chicken yelled.

Lisa turned to him. "Don't say *shut up.* It's very rude."

"Fine," the rubber chicken said. **"BE QUIET!"**

So Nate and Lisa were very quiet. They whispered, "Does not, does so, does not, does so, does not, does so, does not, does so," for about half an hour, which was at least as annoying as a barking dog.

"Yo!" Ed said. "I hate to interrupt your fascinating conversation. But do you notice anything?"

"Yes. You're really grumpy, Ed," Lisa said.

"And you still smell bad," Nate added.

"I meant did you notice anything about your mutt?" Ed asked.

The dog lay on the ground on her back, her furry legs sticking up in the air.

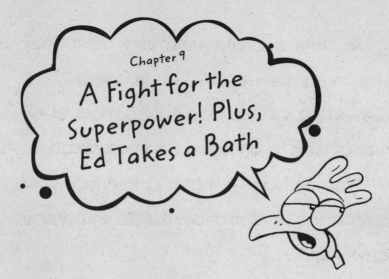

Chapter 9

A Fight for the Superpower! Plus, Ed Takes a Bath

Lisa kneeled over the dog. "Poor Ploppy! Is she all right? Is she alive?"

Nate pressed Plop's front paw. "I can't feel a pulse."

"But I can smell Plop's dog breath. Woowee!" Lisa exclaimed. "It smells a bit like Mrs. Crabpit's breath on a good day. Plop is definitely alive. She needs about a gallon of mouthwash, but she's alive."

"Psst!" Ed hissed. "Message for the clueless: your mutt is resting. Having super strength uses up a lot of energy. So, do you know what that means?"

"She won't bark anymore," Lisa said.

"She won't run around or tear holes in the backyard anymore," Nate said.

"And?" Ed asked. "What else?"

Lisa and Nate stared at the chicken.

"The spell wore off," Ed said. "Sheesh! Do I have to explain everything?"

"I get it," Lisa said. "Now that Plop's super strength has worn off, someone else can have a superpower. Someone who really deserves it."

"Like Benny, to make him smarter," Nate said.

"Like Ashley, to make her less shy," Lisa said.

"Benny," Nate said.

"Ashley," Lisa said.

"Benny."
"Ashley."
"Benny."
"Ashley."
"SHUT–" Ed screamed.

"Watch your language," Lisa interrupted him.

"Okay, then. **BE QUIET!"**

Ed sighed. "I never, ever thought I'd say this. But after listening to you two, I actually miss Dave." He sighed. "It was so much easier with just one owner. Of course, I've had worse. In the early '80s, I was owned by all five starters for the Celtics. They could never agree on what superpowers to wish for."

Nate's eyes bulged. "You were owned by the Boston Celtics basketball team?"

"No. The Cincinatti Celtics Irish dancing team," Ed said. "They were nice little girls, except when they lost a competition. Then they acted like big crankypants. And don't even get me started on the McFarble quadruplets."

"Now, about my friend Ashley," Lisa said. "I would like to help her become less shy."

"And I want my friend Benny to be smarter," Nate said.

"Since I have the magic, I'll settle this," Ed said. "First come, first served. And Lisa found me first tonight."

Nate crossed his arms. "Hey that's not—"

Lisa interrupted her brother. "Ed, I order you to give the first person who touches you super charm."

"But that's not fair," Nate said.

"She beat you, bub," Ed said. "You'll just have to wait your turn. I can take care of only one wish at a time, and Lisa goes first. So, super charm it is."

"Hooray!" Lisa squealed.

"There's just one problem," the rubber

chicken said. "I don't know what super charm is."

"Of course you don't. You don't have *any* charm," Nate told him.

"I think you have a little bit, Ed," Lisa said. "Maybe. Sometimes."

"So tell me what it is, already," Ed said.

"Super charm means that when Ashley opens her mouth tomorrow, she won't have any trouble talking. She'll say charming things," Lisa told the chicken. "She'll sound nice and smart and funny, and everyone will want to listen."

"Oh, now I get it," Ed said. "Tomorrow, your shy friend Ashley will be sweet-talking everyone around her."

"Exactly! Thanks," Lisa said.

"Just don't let your mutt touch me again. I have no interest in hearing a talking dog," Ed said. "Especially not yours."

Plop let out a loud snore.

"Don't worry. I'm going to keep you safe." Lisa held the rubber chicken tightly against her chest. Then she plugged her nose and said, "Eww. You really need a bath, Eddie."

"The name is Ed," the chicken corrected her. "And I'd rather have a shower."

"A bath it is then, Eddie," Lisa said. "I can't wait to take you to school tomorrow and have Ashley touch you first thing."

Nate kicked his foot hard in the dirt. He hit a hole and fell on his face.

He lifted his head, spit out some of the dirt he'd swallowed, and muttered, "It's so unfair that you get the first wish, Lisa."

"Life's unfair," Lisa said. "I smell food." She returned to the house with Ed.

Nate followed her.

While they waited for their mother to cook dinner, Lisa gave Ed a bubble bath.

Ed complained about the water being too cold, then too hot, then too cold. Ed also shrieked whenever the water got near his eyes, said he didn't like the shampoo scent, and whined that the washcloth was too scratchy.

Lisa didn't quit. "My friend Ashley won't want to touch a dirty rubber chicken. And

I really want to give her super charm," she said. "Besides, Eddie, you're kind of cute when you're covered in soap bubbles."

"Get me out of here," the chicken said.

So Lisa did. After about an hour, anyway.

Then she brought Ed to her bedroom. She tucked him under her frilly pink bedspread, between her teddy bear Toodles and her Peepee Patsy doll.

"Patsy better not have any potty accidents," Ed said.

"Don't worry," Lisa said. "If you get dirty, I can always give you another bath."

Ed groaned. "Life with the McFarble quadruplets doesn't seem so bad, after all."

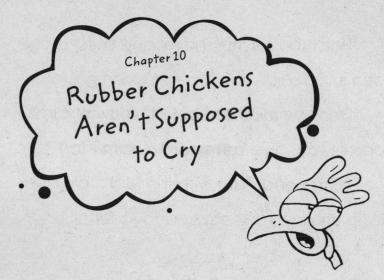

Chapter 10

Rubber Chickens Aren't Supposed to Cry

The next morning, Lisa put Ed into her pretty pink princess backpack, rubber feet first. "Once we're out in public, you can't talk," she told him. "People might think a talking rubber chicken is valuable and try to steal you."

"As my owners," he said, "you and Nate are the only ones who can hear me. Duh!"

"Phew! That's a relief," Lisa said. "But no need to be rude about it."

She stuffed his head down and zipped up her backpack.

"**Let me Out!**" the rubber chicken squawked. "It's dark and creepy in here. I hate this!"

Lisa sniffed. "Well, I hate the way you're making my pretty pink princess backpack look bulky. But don't worry, Eddie. I'll let you out as soon as I see my friend Ashley."

"Just get me to this Ashley chick," Ed said.

"She's a girl, not a chick," Lisa said.

"Girl, chick, whatever. Move it."

"Didn't you mean to say please?" Lisa asked.

"Okay, **please!**" Ed yelled. "Sheesh!"

"You don't have to yell," Lisa said. Then she yelled, "**Nate! Time for school!**"

Nate trudged down the stairs, his backpack slung over one shoulder. "I can't believe you got to make the first wish," he told Lisa.

"Well, believe it," she said.

"And super charm?" Nate shook his head. "Of all the superpowers in the world, you had to make Ashley talk nicely. That's super lame-o."

"Ashley will appreciate it," Lisa said.

"You could have made her fly, or given her x-ray vision, or invisibility. But no-o-o. You had to let her talk nicely."

"Speaking of talking nicely, will you two chill out!" Ed shouted from inside the backpack. "You two argue even more than me and my brothers Ned and Ted."

"Rubber chickens have brothers?" Nate asked.

"Not all of us," Ed said. "Some of us have sisters. Besides my brothers Ned and Ted, I have a sister, Winifred. And there's my goldfish Jed." His voice was raspy. "I really miss them."

"Oh, poor Eddie!" Lisa said. "I hate to hear you cry!"

Ed sniffed a bunch of times. "I wasn't crying," he said. "Don't you have to get to school or something?"

"Yes! We'd better hurry to the bus stop," Lisa said. "We wouldn't want to be late."

"Speak for yourself," Nate mumbled.

But he walked with Lisa toward the front door. They called out, "Bye, Mom!"

Their mother stopped typing. "Wait," she said. "I still need a name for the dog in my new book. Something old-fashioned. The Newbery committee likes that sweet, whole-some stuff. Sounder? No. Winn-Dixie? No."

"Does your mother ever think about any-thing besides her books?" the chicken asked.

"Ed, please," Lisa warned.

"You want to name the dog Ed?" their mother asked. "That's brilliant! Ed! Very old-fashioned. It's positively Edwardian! Remind me to give you a penny when I win the Newbery award for *The Sad Saga of Ed, the Doomed Dog*."

She kept talking, even after the twins had left the house and boarded the school bus.

Chapter 11
Ed Goes to School

Nate rode in the back of the school bus. His friend Michael sat across the aisle from him and tutored him in the art of fake farts.

Lisa sat next to a third-grader in the front row. She wanted to be first off the bus so she could give her friend Ashley super charm right away.

Lisa's backpack, with Ed inside it, rested on the bus floor between her feet.

"I feel sick!" Ed yelled. "And your pointy shoes keep knocking into me. Agh!"

"Relax. We'll be there soon," Lisa told the rubber chicken.

The girl next to her tilted her head. "Are you talking to me?"

Lisa wasn't about to say she was talking to a supernatural rubber chicken. So she nodded instead.

"I guess you can tell I'm scared about my spelling test today. Okay, I'll try to relax," the girl said. "Thanks for your concern."

Lisa smiled. "You're welcome."

"Concern!" Ed shouted. "You're only concerned about yourself. You couldn't care less about a helpless old bird, could you? No one cares about me. Wah! I feel tears building up behind my beady eyes."

"Oh, little chicken," Lisa said in a gentle voice.

Lisa's seatmate said, "It's not nice to call me a little chicken just because I'm scared of a spelling test."

"I feel sick inside your dorky princess backpack," Ed whined.

"You sure complain a lot," Lisa complained.

The girl next to her said, "How rude!"

The bus lurched to a halt in front of the school.

"I wasn't talking about you complain—" But before Lisa could finish the sentence, the girl stomped off the bus.

Lisa picked up her backpack, unzipped it, and looked in.

"Are you okay now?" she asked the rubber chicken.

"That was the worst ride I ever had," Ed said. "Even worse than being in Dave's old truck with his wetsuits and surfboards. At least he never shoved me in a backpack. You should have more respect for your fine feathered friends."

"You don't even have feathers," Lisa said. "And if you did, I bet they wouldn't be fine."

"Plus, I'm not your friend," Ed added.

"That's not a nice thing to say." Lisa zipped up her backpack again, muffling Ed's voice. She put the pack on her shoulders.

Unfortunately, that just allowed Ed to talk closer to Lisa's ears. "I'm miserable, I tell you. Miserable," he said.

Lisa sighed. "Why do you have to be so grumpy all the time?" She walked off the bus.

She saw Ashley and some other students waiting outside the classroom door. Lisa whispered, "Ed, there's my shy friend Ashley Chang. The black-haired girl, with her head down and her cheeks flushed. The one who's not saying a word while the kids around her jabber away. Do you see her?"

"Newsflash," Ed said. "I can't see your pal Ashley or anything else. It's completely dark inside this backpack."

"Oh, right. I'll take you out so you can look at her," Lisa said. "Besides, I need to get her to touch you. This is going to be so great! Soon Ashley will be super charming. She'll talk so well today, she'll never feel shy again. Here we go!"

Chapter 12

Super Oops

Lisa took off her pretty pink princess backpack, held it by one of the straps, and slowly unzipped it.

"Well, it's about time," the rubber chicken said. "Do you know how horrible it is being stuck inside a backpack? I felt like one of those poor magic genies trapped in a bottle for thousands of years. At least a bottle is see-through. It's really dark inside your backpack."

"Sorry," Lisa whispered. "Now will you please stop whining?"

"Excu-u-use me," the chicken said. "Sheesh."

Lisa walked over to Ashley Chang, who stood outside with some of their classmates before school.

Ashley gave Lisa a tiny wave.

"Hi, Lisa," her friend Brittany Billingsworth said.

"How are you doing?" her friend Michelle Bell asked.

"I'm doing great," Lisa said.

"I'm an emotional wreck if you really want to know," Ed whined.

"Be quiet," Lisa said.

"That was a mean thing to say," Michelle said.

"Sorry." Lisa sighed. "Ashley, I want to show you something funny I found."

"Can I see too?" Brittany asked.

"After Ashley, okay?" Lisa grabbed the rubber chicken by the neck and yanked him from her backpack.

"Gross," Brittany said.

"Yuck," Michelle said.

Ashley put her hands over her eyes.

"For your information," Ed squawked, "other rubber chickens find me quite handsome. I'll have you know, my mother was fourth runner-up in the Miss Rubber Chicken contest. Of course, that was in her younger days, when she was a spring chicken."

"You have a mother?" Lisa asked Ed.

"We all have mothers," Michelle said. "Lisa, are you sure you're okay?"

"Uh, I meant that this rubber chicken has a face only a mother could love. But the chicken's necklace is pretty."

"It's not a necklace!" Ed shouted. "It's a Hawaiian lei."

Lisa ignored him. "Feel the necklace, Ashley," she said.

Ashley shook her head.

Lisa thrust the chicken forward, but Ashley backed away, her eyes wide with terror.

"It's just a toy," Lisa pleaded with her friend.

"It's not that," Ashley whispered as she kept moving back.

Suddenly, someone behind Lisa reached out a chubby, grimy hand and grabbed the chicken by his neck.

"**Ow!**" Ed yelled.

Lisa turned around. Hulk Paine was clutching her chicken.

"Look what I found," he said.

"That's mine!" Lisa yelled.

"Finders, keepers." Hulk stuffed the chicken into his evil pirate backpack and closed the zipper.

"Not again!" Ed squawked inside the backpack. "Help! Help! I can't see a thing! Get me out of here!"

Lisa bit her lip. She didn't know what to do. She wanted to help the supernatural rubber chicken, especially since he could help her friend Ashley. But she was terrified of Hulk Paine. She knew he would have no problem punching a girl.

"Help! Please!" Ed shouted inside the backpack. "Pretty please! Pretty please with sugar on top! **GET ME OUT OF HERE!**"

"I'll try," Lisa told him. "But Hulk might punch me."

Hulk shook his head. "Lisa, sweetheart," he said in a sweet, soothing voice, "I would hate to punch a lovely girl like you. I wouldn't want anything bad to happen to such a perfect human being."

"Hulk? Are you feeling all right?" Lisa asked.

"I'm fine. Now that I'm in your presence. Speaking of presents, spending time with you is better than Christmas and my birthday combined."

Lisa tilted her head. "What is wrong with you? Last year at Christmastime, you ran around saying 'Bah, humbug' to everyone and trying to steal their gifts."

"Things have changed, my lovely Lisa. And speaking of change, I love your new hairdo. It's divine."

"Now I really feel like throwing up," Ed said. "It's horrible enough in this dark, evil pirate backpack without hearing you being called divine."

"Oh, no!" Lisa exclaimed. She knew why Hulk Paine was talking strangely. "Hulk, you touched my rubber chicken."

"Yes, and what a darling little chicken it is," he said.

"Darling?" Ed said. "Yuck! You may call me handsome or gorgeous, but not darling. Little baby rubber chickies are darling. Except for my cousin Sidney, who has always been ugly, even as a young chick. But I'm not a baby. So don't call me darling, you big lug."

"That rubber chicken is almost as darling as you are, Lisa," Hulk said.

Lisa clutched her racing heart as she realized what had happened. Hulk had touched the rubber chicken, and that meant only one thing: she had accidentally given Hulk Paine—the biggest bully in fourth grade—super charm.

Chapter 13
The Incredible Hulk

After perfecting his fake farts on the school bus, and then beating his friend Benny in a fake fart contest, Nate decided to check whether Ashley had gotten the gift of super charm.

He walked toward her, and Benny followed him.

As Nate got close to Ashley, he called out, "How's it going?"

She opened her mouth, but no sounds came out.

Nate stopped a few inches from her. "I didn't catch that. How's it going, Ashley?"

"Fine," she whispered. Ashley didn't sound like she had the gift of super charm, or any other gift except super shyness. Shyness seemed like a gift most people would want to return to the store and exchange for something better, like a video game or a book or even a pair of socks.

"I'm so glad to hear you're doing fine," Hulk Paine said to Ashley. "A sweet girl like you deserves the best."

Nate waited for Hulk to say an insulting punch line. But he didn't.

Instead, Hulk slapped Nate on the back, sending him flying.

Nate landed face first on the lawn.

"I'm so sorry," Hulk said. "I don't realize my own strength sometimes. Please forgive me."

Nate spit out a twig, a mouthful of grass, and a live worm. Then he stared at Lisa with his eyebrows raised halfway to the top of his head.

"Hulk touched the rubber chicken before anyone else could get to it," Lisa explained. "Now he's super charming."

Nate's eyebrows moved all the way to the top of his head.

"I just couldn't resist the adorable birdie," Hulk said.

"Adorable? Agh! I'm not adorable," Ed said from inside Hulk's backpack. "Handsome or gorgeous, remember? But not adorable. And don't call me a birdie either."

"She's such a darling chicken," Hulk said.

"She? She?" Ed exclaimed. "For your information, I'm a boy chicken."

The bell rang, signaling that school would start in five minutes. For once, Nate was actually happy to hear it, because it drowned out Ed's whiny voice.

"Well, I'm off to begin an adventure in learning." Hulk said. "As much as I love being with you wonderful people, I must tear myself away so that I can gain knowledge and become a better human being. Who wants to join me?"

Everybody except Benny B. Benjamin looked away from Hulk. They hoped the method to avoid getting called on in class would also work to avoid walking to class with Hulk Paine. He might seem sweet this morning, but after years of his bullying, his classmates didn't trust him.

"Benny, what about you? I always enjoy

your fine company," Hulk said.

"Oops! I forgot I wasn't supposed to look at you," Benny said. "Are you going to call me dummy today? Or idiot? Or stupid?"

"No way!" Hulk said.

"Not even doofushead?" Benny asked.

"I am not a name-caller," Hulk said. "People insult others because they feel bad about themselves. And anyone who calls someone else a doofushead is a doofushead himself."

"Wow!" Benny said.

"I really think you're quite bright. You just need to realize that yourself," Hulk said.

"Okay, thanks. I guess." Benny shrugged. "I'll go to class with you."

"And how about you, Ashley?" Hulk asked.

She nodded and whispered, "Yes."

"You have such a beautiful voice," Hulk said. "I wish you would use it more."

"We'd better get to class so we won't be late," Benny said.

"How smart of you to realize that," Hulk said. "And Ashley, how brave you are to walk with me."

"Thank you," Ashley said in a voice that was actually louder than a whisper for once.

So Hulk rushed toward class, with Benny and Ashley following him. Hulk's backpack moved up and down and across his big back as he ran.

Inside the backpack, Ed screamed, "Help! **Save me!**"

"You'll be fine!" Nate yelled back.

Hulk stopped and turned his head. "Thank you for encouraging me, Nate. You're so supportive!" He hurried off again, with Ed squawking in his backpack.

"You really messed up your turn with the rubber chicken," Nate told Lisa.

"Maybe I did," Lisa said. "But it's fun to hear Hulk Paine say things like 'You're so supportive.'"

"That's true," Nate said, "I wonder what will come out of Hulk's mouth next."

Chapter 14

The Incredible Hulk
Strikes Again

As soon as school started, Mrs. Crabpit asked for volunteers to solve hard math problems.

Hulk Paine was the first person to raise his hand. Actually, he was the only person to raise his hand. And he kept raising his hand all morning long.

This helped the entire fourth-grade class. Lisa didn't have to look away from the teacher anymore. Ashley Chang's cheeks didn't turn

Mars red. Brittany Billingsworth didn't break out in her usual rash or even an unusual rash. And Michael Perez didn't have to wipe a bunch of sweat off his forehead.

Hulk got most of the answers wrong. Ed's spell obviously hadn't made him smarter. But every time Hulk made a mistake, he apologized in a charming way, making Mrs. Crabpit too happy to be her usual nasty self.

For instance, he told Mrs. Crabpit that her smile was so dazzling, any thoughts of long division had flown right out of his brain. And when Mrs. Crabpit said Hulk was wrong about the pig dying at the end of *Charlotte's Web,* he yelled, "Thank

goodness! Thinking about the wonderful pig's death almost broke my heart."

"Then I won't tell you who really dies at the end of the book," Mrs. Crabpit said.

"It's the spider!" Ed yelled. "She bites the dust, kicks the bucket, goes to the giant spiderweb in the sky. In other words, she dies. The poor dear."

$$28 \overline{)9,756}$$

$$827 \overline{)11,112}$$

Then Hulk did the kindest thing anyone had ever done for Mrs. Crabpit's fourth grade class. He opened up his backpack.

Ed yelled, "I can see again! Yahoo!"

Actually, Hulk's act of opening his back-pack wasn't the kindest thing anyone had ever done for the class.

Wait for it.

Ho hum.
Tra la la.
YAWN.
Zzzzz
WAKE UP! And thanks for waiting.

All right, here comes the kindest thing anyone ever did for Mrs. Crabpit's fourth grade class: Hulk Paine took out a package of fresh-breath mints and offered one to Mrs. Crabpit. He told her, "I like you so much that I want to share my very favorite mints with my very favorite fourth grade teacher."

Mrs. Crabpit was so excited by Hulk's compliment that she forgot she was his only fourth grade teacher.

"Thank you, Hulk," she said before popping the fresh-breath mint into her mouth.

The whole class, together, breathed a sigh of relief.

Nate passed a note to Hulk that said:

Thanks, big guy.

Later, could you try to get her to take a shower too?

From,

Nate Zupinski

Hulk wrote back:

Dear Nate Zupinski,
Great idea, pal!
Thank you for your excellent suggestion.
Smooches!
Your pal,
Hulk Paine

Hulk returned the package of breath mints to his backpack and closed the zipper again.

Ed screamed, "**NO-O-O! Get me out of here! I hate the dark!**"

But everyone else was happy.

Nate and Lisa were especially happy that Ed's whiny voice was muffled inside the closed backpack again.

Chapter 15
How Special

After the bell rang for recess, Hulk thanked Mrs. Crabpit for an enjoyable morning, held the classroom door open, and said nice things to every student as they passed him. He told Nate that he appeared to have grown at least three inches taller this month. He told Lisa that her dress looked just like one he'd seen on a Hollywood awards show last night, except that hers was prettier.

Ed squawked from inside the backpack, "All this sweetsy talk is making me want to throw up."

"I think it's great," Lisa said.

"Me too," Hulk said. "It is a great dress."

"Barf," Ed said.

"Don't be so grumpy," Lisa told Ed.

Hulk tilted his head. "Am I upsetting you? I'm sorry, darling Lisa."

"Are you really Hulk Paine?" Benny B. Benjamin asked him at the doorway. "You seem so nice."

"I understand how a smart kid like you could have trouble believing I'm really me," Hulk said.

Benny scratched his head. "Huh?"

"Exactly," Hulk said.

"Uh, yeah," Benny muttered as he rushed out of the classroom.

When Ashley came through the doorway, Hulk asked her, "Would you be a dear and make sure sweet old Benny is okay? He looked a bit upset as he left. He needs to hear your soothing voice."

"Since you think Benny needs my help, I'll try to talk to him," Ashley promised Hulk.

Hulk stayed at the open doorway to chat with everyone on their way to recess. He had to wait a long time for Dan the Dawdler, who still had to put away his binder, tie his shoes, and think about the meaning of life.

Outside on the playground, Ashley came

up to Benny and whispered, "Are you all right?"

Benny scratched his head again. Then he tried to talk, but he couldn't scratch his head and talk at the same time. So he stopped scratching his head. He asked Ashley, "Do you think aliens stole Hulk Paine and replaced him with a nice guy?"

Ashley laughed. "You're so witty."

"And you're talking. You sound good," Benny said. "Hey, as long as you're finally using your voice, could you explain the math homework to me?"

Ashley nodded. **"I mean, YES, I CAN,"** she said loudly. **"I'll be glad to explain the answers I got."**

"That would be really helpful," Benny said.

"It also would help me," Ashley said. "Hulk Paine thinks I have a soothing voice. So I'm going to try to talk more from now on. Helping you with math should give me good practice."

"Hulk Paine told me I'm smarter than I think I am," Benny said. "Or something like that."

They smiled at each other as they walked to their backpacks to get their homework.

Nate and Lisa smiled too as they watched Benny and Ashley together.

So did Hulk. "How special!" he called out.

Chapter 16

A Perfect Ending, Sort Of

Nate and Lisa walked over to Hulk.

He stood at the entrance to the classroom. He was still waiting for Dan the Dawdler, who was tying his shoe in a quadruple knot.

"I'm glad you've been so charming today," Lisa told Hulk.

"Me too," Hulk said. "I learned a valuable lesson."

"Not to wait for Dan the Dawdler?" Nate asked.

"Well, that too," Hulk said. "But also that if I'm kind to people, they'll be kind to me." He smiled.

Lisa smiled back at him. "So, Hulk, sweetheart," she said. "Tomorrow, you might not be in such a good mood. You may even feel that you've lost your super charm. Will you try to remember to speak nicely to people?"

"I'll try not to forget."

"And before you forget about my rubber chicken, could you please return him to me now?" Lisa asked.

"You tell him, girlie!" Ed squawked from inside the backpack.

"Of course, my dear friend Lisa," Hulk said.

"Anything for you."

Lisa put out her hand, waiting for Hulk to hand over the chicken.

"But I'm afraid it will cost you five dollars," he said.

"What?" Nate asked. "I thought you were a nice guy now, Hulk."

"I *talk* nicely now. That doesn't mean I *am* nice. Please give me the money, and the rubber chicken is all yours."

Lisa frowned.

Nate sighed.

"Oh, dear," Hulk said. "You're not cooperating with me. Well, if you don't want the rubber chicken, I can keep him. I've grown quite fond of the darling toy."

"But I haven't grown fond of you, you big brute," Ed said.

Lisa got out her pretty pink princess backpack, took out her pink polka dot petunias wallet, found a five-dollar bill, and gave it to Hulk.

He returned the rubber chicken to her.

"It's about time!" Ed exclaimed.

"Oh, shut up," Lisa said.

"Is that any way to talk?" Hulk asked.

"Yeah," Ed said. "Is that any way to talk?"

Lisa shook her head. There was nothing worse than being scolded by both Hulk Paine and an obnoxious rubber chicken.

Actually, getting crushed by a giant boulder or flattened by a high-speed train would probably be worse.

But, still, Lisa didn't like Hulk and Ed scolding her.

"You're rude," Hulk said to Lisa. "I'm going to walk over there." He pointed to the lunch table where Ashley sat next to Benny, trying to explain subtraction to him.

"Are you going to help them learn math?" Nate asked.

"Nope. I'm going to ask them to donate their valuables to me. Remember, I may have super charm, but I'm still a big bully."

Once Hulk left, Nate said, "Giving Hulk super charm was totally lame."

Ed frowned. "Are you calling my super-natural powers lame?"

"You should have let me make the first wish," Nate said. "I was going to give Benny super smarts so he'd get more confident and do better in school."

"My spells are not lame," Ed said. "Look at your friends now."

The twins turned toward Ashley and Benny.

"Ha!" Lisa told Nate. "My wish worked just fine on both Ashley and Benny. And even on Hulk Paine too. What a perfect ending!"

"Told you so," Ed said to Nate.

Hulk walked up to Ashley and Benny. "You are smart, Benny. And Ashley, I'm so glad you're talking. Now, my darlings, please give me all your money. Bills are best, but coins are fine too. Also, I'd like any jewelry you're wearing, especially if it's gold."

"I guess the spell didn't work so well on Hulk," Lisa admitted.

"Maybe. Maybe not," Ed said. "Listen to your friends now."

Ashley was loudly telling the playground monitor that Hulk was trying to steal from them.

Then Benny smartly explained that theft by extortion was illegal under the Arizona Criminal Code.

The playground monitor made Hulk return Lisa's five dollars before sending him to the principal's office.

"You see?" the rubber chicken said. "Always remember: Sometimes things don't seem to be working out, but they really do in the end. Lisa's wish brought your friends together. They just needed to help each other realize how special they are."

"Hey, Ed," Lisa said. "You're really sweet, in your own way." She smiled.

"And for a rubber chicken, you're pretty smart," Nate added. He smiled too.

"When we get home, I'm going to give you an extra-long bath, with lots of bubbles!" Lisa said.

The supernatural rubber chicken groaned. "And you wonder why I'm so grumpy."